HACKING THE CODE

The Ziggety Zaggety Road
of a D-Kid

By Gea Meijering

Illustrated by Mads Johan Øgaard

iCare
PRESS

ISBN: 978-1-7366261-0-8

[1.Elementary Schools - Fiction. 2.Friendship - Fiction. 3.Humorous Stories - Fiction. 4.Learning Disabilities - Fiction. 5.Dyslexia - Fiction.]

Summary: When Kees, a creative prankster, pulls off another prank at school (a rather good one), the Principal gives him an unusual and for him impossible punishment. He has to write a two-page essay about the hardest thing he has ever done. That's a big problem because he is no good at writing. He's dyslexic. Will he be able to pull it off? And how on earth did he end up with the highest honor of the entire elementary school after all that happened?

Cover design by Mads Johan Øgaard and Gea Meijering
Interior design by Gea Meijering

Library of Congress Cataloging-in-Publication Data has been applied for and may be obtained from the Library of Congress.

iCarePress books are available at special discounts when purchased in quantity for premiums and promotions as well as fundraising or educational use. For details, contact icarepress@gmail.com or www. icarepress.com.

iCare
PRESS

For you....

and everyone with a learning difference.

1
Strike One

"Not so fast, Bobby."

Mom scrambles out the door behind my little brother.

"Yeah, Bobble. You don't have to be the first at school ALL the time!"

I'm following in my mom's tracks, trying not to explode. My little brother always has to be first.

First into class.

First to finish making his lunch in the morning.

First to tie his shoes.

First to finish his homework.

First to read a book.

First in EVERYTHING!!!

It's really annoying.

Bobble can be so irritating with his pencil behind his ear and a book in his hand, looking like Mr. Smartypants.

I call him Bobble. Kind of like Bobby, but more annoying.

What bothers me most is that he's lightyears ahead of me in reading. I'm in fifth grade, he's in third - and while I'm barely able to get through a page (without pictures) in a day, he's talking about all the chapters he's read, every single night. The bookworm.

As usual, I'm staying as far away from him

and Mom as I can because I always pick up my best friend, Pete, on my way to school. And I don't want Bobble interfering.

We live two doors down from each other, which is the best thing ever.

Pete and I have known each other from way back when we played together in the sandbox. Unlike me, he is never worried about anything. Most of the time, Pete is kicking a soccer ball around his front yard when I come to pick him up for school, which is exactly what he's doing today.

"Yo, Kees! What's up with your socks today?"

Pete catches the ball with his feet and smiles.

"Just for you, I'm wearing one with Ajax's team colors - red with white stars." Ajax is a Dutch soccer team, and Pete's favorite. I could have said that the red and white was for the Angels, a baseball team, but Pete prefers soccer.

I started wearing a different sock on each foot ever since we had a quiz on left and right. It's impossible for me to remember which is which. And believe me, I've tried.

So, in the end, I decided to wear a *red* sock with rockets on my *right* foot and one with *lightbulbs* on my *left* foot for the quiz. It worked, and ever since, I wear a different sock on each foot. It's kind of my signature look.

Pete and I have been in the same class a couple times. I don't know what I would have done without him. We are a great team. If there's a group project, we always try to do it together. If the teacher lets us, that is. Pete is good at writing things up. I'm not - but I *am* good at making things, which Pete isn't. He's got two left hands.

Like the volcano project from papier mâché in fourth grade. I made the volcano, and Pete wrote the journal about the project.

We also stick up for each other in handball disputes. Not to mention, we love to play a good prank.

Like last week, right after school. After most people had left, we decided it was the perfect time for a good trick. We tied an old wallet onto a long fishing line, then put a few dollar bills in it, sticking out just far enough to show a little. We tossed the wallet on the sidewalk and hid behind the bushes.

Sure enough, our principal, Mr. Lamares, walked out. Oh, yeah! He saw the wallet and bent forward to pick it up. *Yank!* Pete pulled the string, and Mr. Lamares reared back looking like he saw a cockroach. Pete had to hold his hand over my mouth to smother my laugh.

We actually would have been better off

running away, but we had to reel in our money first. However, we underestimated our principal's base-jumping skills as he easily jumped on the sliding wallet.

He grabbed the wallet, tugged on the fishing line, and sneered, "Okay, show yourself if you want your money back."

Oh, man!

Unfortunately, this was not the first time we met the principal in a surprising way. (The first time was because of our glue stick incident. That was when we catapulted all the glue sticks we could find at the classroom ceiling, making it look like an icicle cave. Yep, we've always got a lot of fun going on.)

"Ah, here we have our infamous duo," he said. "Let me guess, Kees had this marvelous idea and Pete provided the cash?"

Off we marched into the principal's office (again). Our parents had to pick us up, and we got lunchtime trash duty for a week, which actually wasn't that bad. I can think of worse things, like staying in during breaks, which would kill me. I really need to blow off steam and run free after a morning in class trying to read and write, which is like hacking code for me. It's like impossible for me to decipher what it says on a page as fast as the rest of the class and even harder for me to write. I am doing it letter by letter.

Anyway, I'd take trash duty over missing recess any day, but I am not going to be the one to tell Mr. Lamares, and let's hope he never finds out!

2
Apple or Android Brain?

By the way, I didn't properly introduce myself. My name is Kees. Not like "keys" but more like "case." Yep, that's my name. My parents had a real "aha!" moment when I was born. The doctors and nurses had to put me in a plastic hospital bin for a second while they checked to see if my mom was ok.

And after that was all resolved, their attention went back to me. But I was so quiet, they couldn't remember... where did they leave the baby? Really. I was in a plastic CASE. Hence my name.

Actually, I'm kidding. My grandpa's name is Kees, so there you have it... Oh, and I love telling stories.

I was born with an Apple brain. "A what?" you

say. No, no, my head didn't look like an apple.
It was actually a very definite cone shape at first.

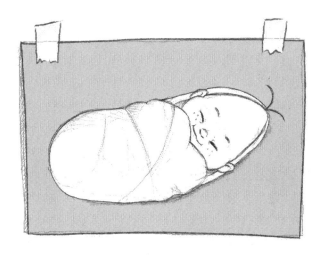

Not that I remember anything about that;
phew, good thing. But my parents have a pretty
telling photo. Luckily, it changed fast. You
should ask your parents about your head shape
when you were born. It might surprise you. I bet
that question hasn't crossed your mind lately? Or
ever?

So, why do I label my brain as an Apple
brain? It has to do with the inner workings. There

are two types of brains in my world. I call them Apple brains and Android brains. Yes, like the smartphones.

Let me explain.

From the outside, you think all smartphones work the same. But if you want to switch phones and need to upload everything, like your old text messages, apps, photos, and contacts, to the other type of phone, it's not that easy. You have probably heard this from someone who wanted to switch phones, like your parents, an uncle - or maybe you switched yourself? These two types of phones use a different code to process everything. You can't run an Apple code on an Android phone, and vice versa.

In a similar way, my brain doesn't process "Android" stuff, like text, instructions, or numbers, very well. My brain is better at decoding pictures and designs and 3D things.

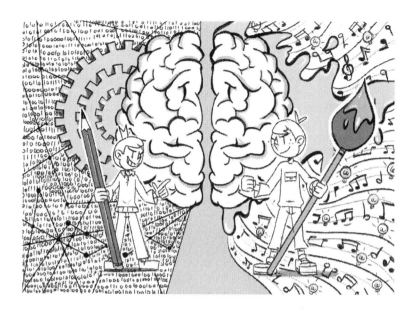

That's also why I have a lot of lightbulb moments. I think and dream up a lot of things in pictures. It's all in me and just keeps flowing out in many different shapes and forms. I can picture it in my head really well before I draw it, make it, tell about it, or write it.

My mom and dad sometimes can't keep up with me and my ingenious plans and inventions, and the same can be said for my teachers. That gets me into a lot of trouble at times. A lot!

But I love it. Never a dull moment in my house.

When I grow up, I want to be an inventor or designer or someone that builds cool things. Or I am going to start my own company and make things that everyone loves. Or...

Not too fast, Kees. Hit the brakes.

Look, I am daydreaming again... If I want to have my own company, first I have to get through school. And my Apple brain isn't made for school.

I know that ending elementary school with straight A's is not in the cards for me. It feels really crappy, really, to always be the last in class to finish an assignment just because it's taking me so long to decode everything. I really am doing the best I can, but unfortunately for me, there's no grade for "trying" in my report cards.

3
Read out Loud!

Pete and I always try to sit together in class every year. In the back of the class where I feel safe and hope I won't be called on too often.

But at the beginning of this school year, our fifth grade teacher separated us within a week. It was a total bummer. I guess our reputation got ahead of us. It's not because we talk all the time. Especially not compared to Sophie and Maria's group, which is like a chicken coop. *Tok, tok, tok. Bla, bla, bla.*

Mrs. Donow claps her hands.

"Kids, today we are going to start with a writing assignment. I want you to write down ten things that make you happy."

I look around and see Sophie and Maria start

to whisper.

"What makes you happy?" I hear Maria say.

I look at Pete and want to ask him the same thing. But before I can open my mouth, the teacher's on top of me.

"On your own, Kees," she says.

The girls start giggling and continue to whisper. It's unbelievable that Mrs. Donow has no reaction to that.

"Ok, kids. What have you got?" Mrs. Donow says after ten minutes. "Who wants to share their list?"

As usual, Maria and Sophie raise their hands immediately.

"Maria, go ahead."

Mrs. Donow likes to ask the girls first most of the time, which we, the boys, really don't mind. But she also praises the girls much more. As if these know-it-all chatterboxes need that. They think they are smarter, funnier, and prettier than the whole world. Well, they're not! But it sure feels that way sometimes.

Maria reads her list of ten things that make her happy. "Dancing, friends, music, laughing, watching a movie, ice cream, shopping, reading, writing, and school."

"Wonderful, Maria! You really thought this through. Great list."

After that, it's Sophie's turn and then finally Tom.

Of course, I don't have ten things written down and am not asked to share them either. Thankfully.

Instead, something worse happens.

"It's time to read out loud, kids."

Every time Mrs. Donow searches for a volunteer to read out loud, I slide down in my chair as far as I can.

My head hits the back of the chair and my chin sits on the table. Put an apple in my mouth and I am like a centerpiece on a medieval serving plate.

"Get your books out, and let's find out what Stella and Tim find at the end of the secret tunnel. I am so excited!"

Well, I'm not!

"Sophie, do you want to start? We are on page 31."

Sophie starts reading at a fast tempo. Like she's being chased by a bulldog. While she is reading, I am counting paragraphs to guess where it's going to be my turn to read.

Mrs. Donow always goes around the room the same way, so I try to decipher the paragraph two pages ahead. That way, when it's my turn, I have seen it before and that helps me a ton. If there's a picture on the page, that's even better. I can make sense of it much better with a picture next to the text.

Meanwhile, it's Pete's turn to read. Pete starts.

"Page 33, at the top."

"You don't have to say that," Mrs. Donow notes. But I know he's doing it for me so I can check where we are. Pete flashes through his paragraphs with ease.

"Kees, your turn."

I can feel my face flushing and my palms getting sweaty.

Here we go.

"Mo-l-es? What – do mo-les – have – to – do – with – a – ny – th – ing – S ss – t ee – ll – a, fro – w – nin."

I hear a giggle from the other side of the room.

"Girls," the teacher interrupts me, "stop giggling! Please continue, Kees."

I stutter and pant my way through the paragraph. I feel like an elephant in the swamp, slowly, bit-by-bit, stuck and being suffocated by the mush of letters and words.

Pete is putting his thumbs up. But all I hear are the groans and sighs from the girls. When I peek to the side, I see they are sliding notes to each other. Mrs. Donow notices it, too.

"One moment, Kees. Ladies, what is so important that it has to be communicated right now? Give me those notes."

Maria reluctantly holds up her scribble. The teacher looks at it and frowns.

"Maria and Sophie, you'll be staying in for recess today so we can talk about this."

I look at Pete, and I know we're both thinking the same. Finally, Mrs. Donow is not amused by what the girls just did.

Yes, *justice!*

4
NADMIL

One Saturday morning in September, Pete and I are in my backyard shed.

"Hey, Pete, I've been thinking," I say.

"What about? You look pretty hyped up for this early in the morning," Pete says.

"I want to form a secret friends group. We're all off to middle school next year and probably won't even be in the same classes anymore. But this friends group is going to last forever. I even have a name for it."

"Oh yeah, what is it?"

"NADMIL," I say with a smile.

"NADMIL? What does that mean?" Pete asks.

"Never a Dull Moment in Ladville!" I tell him proudly.

"Ha, ha! Cool, Kees," he says. "I like it."

"So this is my idea, hear me out."

"I am all ears, Kees." Pete looks at me.

"As the founder of this elite group of 'special' friends, I want you to be my co-founder."

"Me? What do I have to do for that?" Pete asks, looking suspicious.

"Nothing, just help me get things started. This is what I've been thinking. Wannabe members have to go through a very rigorous assessment process. Not very many will make it.

We are going to make it really tough. We want to keep it an elite group, after all."

"Hmmm, I like it. So, I don't have to do this assessment thing?" Pete asks.

"No. You are my co-founder, so you don't," I say.

"Ok, sounds good." Pete looks relieved.

"But anyone who wants to be admitted to NADMIL has to come up with an original prank or skit that doesn't involve spending money. They CAN do something to earn money, which will then go into the NADMIL pot. But there is NO way anyone can buy themselves into NADMIL," I rattle on. "Only an original spoof, not seen or heard before, will do. And the aspiring member has to execute it themselves."

"Wow, you've really thought this out, Kees." Pete is flabbergasted.

"There's more," I continue. "Not everyone can apply. Potential members are invited to apply and are not allowed to talk to anyone about it. If they do so, they are out before they're even in. That also counts for you, Pete!"

"Ok, got it. My lips are sealed. Do you have any idea who you would like as a member?"

"I have a few in mind," I say. "I think our new members should show some creativity, flair, have a can-do mentality, and be kind to others. On the flipside, we will never invite anyone to NADMIL who is constantly giggling, is a nagger, a bully, tattletale, or a teacher's pet. Those people are never going to be aware, EVER, that there is such a thing as NADMIL.

The goal of our club is to become best friends, help each other, and have tons of fun," I continue.

"And we can use this shed as our home base," Pete adds.

"Yes, that's a great idea, Pete! Ok, let's think about potential members."

"Hmm, is it only for boys or also girls?" Pete asks.

"Could be both, as long as they fit into our group. I know a girl who would fit. What do you think about Meghan?"

"I don't know her that well," Pete mumbles. "Shall we think about it?"

"Yes, good idea. But now it's time for ice cream. We have your favorite vanilla chocolate chip in the freezer."

"Bring it on."

5
The Biggest Scare

It only takes a few months into fifth grade before Pete and I have had it with those overly confident, know-it-all, teacher's pets, Sophie and Maria. We start to call them and their following the Sticky Ticks.

Just before Halloween, Mrs. Donow asks us to write about our biggest scare.

"Gosh, I really don't know," Maria boasts.

"I don't get scared easily, actually. Yeah, spiders make me jump, but not those fake spiders."

Pete and I look at each other. I can read his face.

"We can help with that. Yes, we can!" we both say at the same time.

We have an hour to write about our biggest scare before recess, and as usual, I look around me to see everyone else's papers filling up with words, sentences, and paragraphs. Like always, my page stays empty for the longest time.

My head overflows with scary moments, evil plots, plans, tactics, props, locations, costumes... but nothing hits the paper. It's not that I have nothing to write; I just have the hardest time writing something... anything... down. Always.

"Come on, Kees," Mrs. Donow cheers. "You have to try harder."

I SO don't like it when she says that. It's the biggest let-down of all when she says to try harder. Every time I write I AM doing my best. More than that, actually! I am bending over backwards to get something, anything, down on paper. Why doesn't she understand this?

Finally, I manage to get a few sentences on paper.

KEES
(IS bEST)
BIGEST SKARE!

The BIGEST skare foR me saV
Was to finb a cHoped of
nead In the RefRgeReTR At
Home ☺
My head put It terfoRe
My mom but I opend the
cloore First.

Pff, that's all I can do in an hour. Saved by the bell. It's recess.

Pete and I huddle and I come up with a plan on how we can scare those Sticky Ticks.

"Pete, this can be our first NADMIL scheme," I whisper.

"NADMIL?" Pete frowns.

"Yeah, you remember, I told you about

setting up a secret friends group."

"Oh, yeah, but what did NADMIL stand for again?"

"Never a Dull Moment in Ladville."

"Oh, yes, now I remember. Cool, Kees."

"I have some pretty good ideas for our club and more potential members. But first, let's get those Sticky Ticks to scream their heads off."

First, we enlist Meghan, our go-to sidekick. My idea.

She is always game to trick the Sticky Ticks. They've not always been very nice to Meghan, just because she didn't want to go with their girly girl stuff. Meghan is Meghan – with her skateboard and braided hair, she doesn't really fit in their scene. And she doesn't want to, either.

We run to the copy room to sneak out some black poster boards. Then, we cover the window in the boys' bathroom with it.

"Let's test it. Lights out... Yes! It's pitch dark with the door closed. Perfect."

In the meantime, Pete finds some half-empty milk cartons, two of which are sour!

Once we are all set up, Meghan uses her super convincing power to lure the Sticky Ticks to the boys' bathroom. She knocks on the door.

"What's the password?" Pete asks, disguising

his voice. "Viral," she says.

Is she promising the girls the chance to take a video that will go viral? Smart move. They will do anything for attention.

Meghan ushers five girls into the bathroom and closes the door. It is pitch black. Sophie and Maria start to giggle. That is our cue. We jump on the cartons, and BANG!!!!!!!

The four milk cartons EXPLODE, spraying

sour milk throughout the entire bathroom! The acoustics are epic; it sounds like a grenade. And the girls' ear-splitting screams echo through the windows.

The girls are totally, completely, utterly freaked out. And not just by the sound of the "explosion"; they also feel something wet and gooey. It doesn't exactly smell great either, to say the least. More like barf.

"Now you have something scary to write about," I say with a smirk on my face.

That is the last thing that happens before

the campus supervisor opens the door and, well, let's say the school doesn't go on total lockdown because of the "explosion," but it is close. I don't have to tell you that we get into serious trouble because of this. If we weren't already on Mr. Lamares' radar, we certainly are now!

Dang it.

6
New Members

Pete and I discuss new NADMIL members a few times and make a shortlist. We decide that our first invite to apply for a NADMIL membership is to Tom. He was super stoked to hear about NADMIL and really wants to be a part of it.

Now comes the hard part for him: he has to show us that he fits all of the requirements to be a worthy member of the club.

Tom loves to fix things (just like I do), so he goes with that.

At our annual neighborhood garage sale, which happens to be this weekend, Tom sets up shop in his garage.

He sent out flyers and made a sign the day before.

Don't nix it FIX IT

Repair service for everything.
Computers, dolls, lawnmower,
Clothing, glasses etc.

Tom will fix it!

This Saturday at the garage sale.
2496 Venus Road
3D Printer in the house to print parts!

Tom asks us to come with our glue gun. He has equipped the garage with his dad's 3D printer, his mom's sewing machine, his tool kit, and a glue gun.

"Why the glue gun, Tom?" I ask.

"Just in case it gets busy, you can help me. I am always saying, 'If you don't know what to do, just use glue!'"

"Tom, do you know how to work the sewing machine and the 3D printer?" Pete asks him.

"It's not that difficult, guys. My mom taught me how to sew! Because she says I need to be able to fix my own clothes. I tend to rip them pretty easily.

And the 3D printer is actually from my dad. We love making things with it."

Yeah, yeah, I guess we need to see it to believe it.

It is pretty quiet the first hour. We actually don't think this is going to work at all.

"Hey, Tom, you're not going to tell us that we woke up early for nothing? You are raking in negative points."

But finally, he has his first customer, Mr. Brans. He came from the old-age home with a waffle iron that doesn't work anymore.

"Looks like the cable is broken," said Tom, examining it.

With help from his dad, Tom solders the cable back together and then tests the iron. He gets some batter out of the kitchen and makes us all waffles.

Mr. Brans is impressed. "Fantastic!"
"How much do I owe you, Tom?"
"Anything you think it is worth will do."

First off, there is a danger leaving it up to the customer to decide what they will pay you. On one side, the penny-pinchers can give nothing or just peanuts. I mean like, real peanuts. On the other hand, more generous donations are a probability. Tom did make sure there was a $5 bill visible in the cash box to give the payer an idea of the expected range. Very smart of him.

"Ok, here's five dollars, young man."
Whoop, whoop! Five dollars for NADMIL. Good start, Tom.

The next customer is already in line. Mrs. Pranwin from the end of the street travels a lot; we know because there's an airport shuttle in front of her door quite often.

"Hi, Tom. I can't use this suitcase anymore because one clip is broken. It's my favorite suitcase and I'd hate to throw it away. Can you do something about that?"

Tom looks at the clip and searches online. "Ah, here is a 3D drawing of the clip; it's pretty standard. I can 3D print it for you. Maybe it'll work."

"Yes, that would be great!" Mrs. Pranwin exclaims.

While the 3D printer starts printing, Tom fixes a few other easy things.

Tom's neighbor brings in a pair of binoculars that, according to him, don't work anymore. Tom has a look at them, wiggles some dials, and takes them into the garage.

"Ok, now it should work again. Have a look through it. You need to press it firmly against your eyes," Tom says.

And so, Bill the neighbor does. What he doesn't know is that Tom smeared some charcoal around the rims of the binoculars. The neighbor presses really firm and is excited that the binoculars work again. And when he pulls them away, he has a pair of black circles around his eyes. He looks like a panda bear.

"They work again, Tom. Here's three dollars." Ka-chingggg!

Over the rest of the morning, Tom sews a

bag back together, reboots a laptop, cleans up a lawn mower, and installs the clip on Mrs. Pranwin's suitcase. It works! Yeah, another happy customer.

Halfway through the day, Tom's neighbor Bill comes by again to see how things are going. He hasn't noticed his charcoal eyes yet, and I think his wife, Mrs. Baker, is playing along. She is standing at the front door grinning at us.

Right at that time, a reporter from the local newspaper comes by to take a picture of Tom's shop.

I just wish we could see Bill's face when he sees himself in the newspaper. Maybe we can ask Mrs. Baker to make a video of it. That would be hilarious.

In the end, Tom makes $65 for our NADMIL fund. That's more than a 100% improvement to our budget since we had nothing to begin with.

After very serious deliberation between Pete and myself, we decide that Tom has passed the test and is now a member of NADMIL. His plan was original and fun, and he managed to put some serious moolah into our NADMIL pot.

Tom is stoked.

7
Remote Control

Birds are chirping and flowers pop. Spring is in full swing when Pete and I stay at the school's playground to shoot some hoops. We see all of the teachers going into Mrs. Beck's room, so we decided to check out what they were doing.

We sneak up to the room, making sure they don't see us. Guess what they are doing? They are watching TV!!!!!

We are never allowed to watch TV at school! What they were watching looks pretty boring. Mr. Smek yawns so hard we could see his tonsils dance.

So, Pete and I decide to make it a little more fun for them. We check the other classrooms to see if there is a door that has been left open. And yes, of course, the ever-so-forgetful Mrs. Honey left her door open. I sneak inside while Pete holds watch at the door. There it is: the TV remote. Every TV in our school is using the same type. We are going to get this party started!!!

In Mrs. Beck's classroom, the teachers are still watching a woman talk on the big 60-inch flat screen. We point the remote through the little window next to the door and click on 1. *Poof!* There is CNN news. It worked!

Pete and I crack up. "Quiet, shhhhh." We've only just begun.

Mr. Lamares searches for the remote but in the end stands up to change the channel by hand – back to the boring woman talking. All the teachers look a bit surprised, but no one seems alarmed or anything. Not yet! Ha!

"What channel now, Pete?"

"Let's do 6."

"Ok, 6 it is."

We point and push, and bang, there are The Simpsons. We can see Mr. Lamares frowning and wondering, "What's wrong with this TV?"

He stands up to switch it back again. We randomly choose channel 10 next... HGTV. My mom always watches these home makeover shows. Now we can hear the teachers mumbling. We keep on pushing buttons: channel 14, there is Big Bird from Sesame Street. The surprised faces of the teachers and the principal getting more and more annoyed is out of this world funny.

We can't keep ourselves quiet anymore and although we quickly sneak away from the window, we HAVE to look to see their reaction just one more time. And that's where things go wrong. Mr. Smek, who is closest to the door, gets up and flings the door open. We laugh so hard that we don't even realize we are busted.

"Pete and Kees," Mr. Smek says. "Perhaps you know about the malfunctioning TV?"

Mr. Lamares arrives at the door and looks at us with a mixture of surprise, annoyance, and anger.

He points with his long, boney fingers. "You two, to my office, now!"

Back in his office, we have to "explain ourselves." Pete and I have tears in our eyes – not from crying but from laughing. We can't help it. Every time we think about the faces of those teachers and the principal, *whoa*. My belly cramps and I have trouble keeping it together. Which I don't.

Mr. Lamares waits until we calm down. Sitting at his desk, he looks grumpy. But I think for a minute that I do see a sliver of a smile.

"Boys, I don't have to explain to you that this behavior is unacceptable. I have seen you here too many times over the past five years. This does it for me. Your parents are going to get a call from me, and..." He pauses for a moment.

"You know, it's not always easy being the principal."

There is nothing wrong with my imagination. But I don't understand that. He's the boss of the school. ANYTHING he says happens. Sort of. What's hard about that?

"I have to think of a suitable punishment. You already had trash duty several times. And I heard from your classmates, Sophie and Maria, who were here a while ago, that you actually don't mind doing that at all. Knowing this, trash duty will actually not have the right effect. The girls really didn't want to do trash duty so they asked if they could do a writing task instead. Since it was their first time in my office, I let them."

He pauses for a moment to think about it.

"So, we are going to do this. You each are going to write me a two-page essay about the hardest thing you have ever done."

Pete looks at me as if he has just heard that his sister was going to share a room with him.

My face is exploding. Thank you, Sticky Ticks, for giving the principal this idea!

Now it is the principal's turn to laugh at our horrified faces.

"You are fifth graders, so that shouldn't be a problem. I want to see a personal story, and I will be able to tell if you have someone else write it for you. You have two weeks. If it is not on my desk by that time, you are going to spend every lunch break and recess at your desk until it's finished," he says.

"Can I type it instead of using handwriting?" I mutter. I have to ask because my hokey-pokey handwriting is the worst, and I soooo need spellcheck.

Luckily, he says this is ok, but it doesn't change that I still have two pages of writing I have to come up with.

This is the worst thing that has ever happened to me.

It is like he found my weak spot. I can't even get a paragraph on paper; one sentence takes me about an hour. How on earth am I going to write two whole pages in the next two weeks?

8
Pinball

On our way home, we have so much fun reliving our remote control stunt. This will stay fresh in our memories for days, I tell you, months, even years. When Pete and I are super old, we'll share this with our grandkids! No doubt about it. Just as Grandpa has these super cool stories from when he was a kid, I will have mine, too.

By now the principal must have talked to my mom.

Pete is not too worried. He has all A's, and his mom and dad are both at work. So he won't hear anything about it until tonight. And even then, knowing them, they won't make such a big fuss about it.

On the other hand, for me, with my D-average, it will be a whole different story.

"You know, Kees," Pete says, looking at me, "I can help you with the writing part. If you come up with what your essay needs to be about, you can dictate to me, or we can come up with something together."

"Thanks, Pete. Maybe. I am going to think about it."

When we arrive at Pete's house, I shout, "Bye, Pete!" as he goes straight to the soccer ball he left behind this morning.

He always plays a little soccer in the street after school. I'm so envious that he has the time to do that.

For the last 100 yards to my house, I pretend to be a turtle. Taking my time.

Mom is working at her computer in the kitchen nook when I come home. Bobby ran ahead of me on the walk home and is already at the kitchen table reading a book.

"Hi, Kees, how was your day?" Mom asks, looking up from her computer.

"Kees and Pete were at the principal's office today. AGAIN!" Bobby almost screams with a smirk on his face.

"Oh, shut up, Bobble." I throw an evil eye at him. "What do you know about it? You don't know why I was there! Maybe the principal needed us for one of his projects, you little know-it-all!"

"Ok, ok," Mom shushes.

"Bobby, take a snack and go to your room. I want to talk to Kees. Alone!"

Bobby grabs a granola bar and a cup of water and stomps up the stairs.

"Want to tell me about it, Kees?" Mom asks.

So, I tell her the entire story from A to Z. Halfway into my explanation, the rattling noise of a plastic cup bouncing up and down the tile hallway floor stops us. Mom opens the door of the hallway and there is Bobble. Rushing back up the stairs laughing.

"Don't come down before I say so, Bobby," Mom yells.

That pesky little know it all, I think. Now the whole school will know about it tomorrow, for sure.

Mom turns her attention to me again. "Oh boy, never a dull moment with you, Kees. That's a nice task you received from the principal."

"It's a disaster. I can't write that essay. You know me, I hate writing. It's like getting teeth pulled. My head always feels like a pinball machine. Ding, ding, ding, ding, ding. Thoughts bounce around my skull, but I can't seem to get them out on paper.

I can draw my thoughts. Totally fine with that. But writing it down. Nah! It will take forever. My brain is cracking and my stomach hurts, every vein in my body protests. Blocking everything.

It's making me very uncomfortable all the time. Do you know what I mean, Mom? It's like you and Dad filling out your tax papers. I always hear Dad swearing when it's time to do that. It's not something new for you two! Is it? You've done it a million times. And lucky for you that's only once a year."

"I hear you, Kees. Nevertheless, I think Mr. Lamares got you this time. I think he's done with all your pranks. So what kind of essay does he expect from you?"

"Ugh, it's impossible. Two weeks from now, I need to hand in a two-page essay about what was the hardest thing I EVER did! And if I am not done by then, he will keep me in every recess until I finish it. I don't know what is worse. Writing the essay or staying in for recess...

"Maybe if I just write in super big words, like this," I say as I scribble across a piece of paper.

"Do you really think he is going to take that?" Mom asks. She is always so practical.

"Oh, Mom. Please help. Will you help me?"

"I could, but maybe you can try it on your own first. Or ask Pete or your teacher for some pointers. What is Pete going to write about?"

"I dunno."

"Maybe you can start on an idea cloud in your notebook with things you might want to write about."

"Ok, that's a good idea."

I grab my notebook out of my backpack and open an empty page.

"The hardest thing I ever did," I write on the top line. Then.......... nothing. Aggh!

First, a little bit of Xbox. I need to cool down. Breathe in, breathe out.

9

Teacher Talk

The next day at recess, Mrs. Donow asks me to stay behind for a moment.

"I heard about your stunt yesterday."

"Oh that," I answer nonchalantly.

"Yes, and what a very fitting task you and Pete received from Mr. Lamares. He asked me to touch base with you a few times this coming week. Do you know what you are going to write about?"

After the talk with my Mom yesterday, I hadn't exactly been thinking about it. I'd rather put it as far away in my mind as I possibly can. Or actually, I don't want it there at all. But that's sort of hard because it's already there. Darn.

"Mr. Lamares told us to write a two-page essay about the hardest thing I ever did."

"Do you have any ideas what to write about?" Mrs. Donow asks.

"Do you?" I ask her.

"Well, Kees, it's your story. Maybe try to tell the principal something that he doesn't already know about you."

I've been in his office so many times. I know exactly what pictures and photos he has hanging on the wall. I know when he has changed something, like a few weeks ago when he switched around the pictures of his daughter.

It's kind of a weird thing that I notice these unimportant things. I have a photographic memory for some things, which is usually handy, but not right now.

"What do I think is hard that he might not suspect? That I hate school?"

"Oh really? Do you really hate school? That is not my impression," Mrs. Donow says.

"I understand that spelling and writing are not your favorite things to do, but you seem to like our STEM hour, or when we figure out how something works. And you are always such a great help when technology lets me down.

Not to mention recess, PE, and art class."

"Yeah, yeah, I guess you're right," I say with a nod. "Can I go out now?" This has taken waaay too much time from my recess.

"Yes, you can go. I'm here to help you, you know that, Kees?"

10
Spelling Test

That Friday evening I go over to Pete's house for dinner. I always like eating there because his mom's spaghetti with meatballs is the best. And, because it's Friday, I don't have to worry about any stupid homework.

Except, by the time I go home, it's all I can think about. Pete's mom had hung his perfect spelling test on the fridge. That will never happen for me, no matter how much I practice my spelling.

For Pete that isn't an issue. He's got the Android brain. He's always playing soccer after school and only needs to glance over his spelling words before the spelling test.

And he always aces the test. ALWAYS. What's even worse? If you make 6 out of 10, or higher, on your spelling test, you get to participate in Friday Funday. Guess who has never participated in Friday Funday? Yup. Yours truly. And then there's the "read out loud" spelling test results each week. The teacher announces what your score is... to the entire class!

"Pete, 10 out of 10,

Meghan, 9 out of 10,

Maria, 10 out of 10,

Tom, 7 out of 10,

Kees, 2 out of 10!"

Aghh!!

Homework is the worst invention ever. The moron who thought about that should be benched. What was he thinking? Let's have these kids go to school all day and then let them repeat the same baloney at home? As if the time at school isn't enough.

Anyway, I'm stuck with it, so I'm usually in my room gazing out the window attempting to do homework while I see Pete and the other kids from the neighborhood playing soccer on the street.

Man, I could put an infinite amount of time into learning my spelling words and still have a D. I've tried everything, and I mean EVERYTHING, to get those words to stick in my head. I've written them out in crayon, chalk on the wall, pencils (of course), but also shaving cream in the bathroom, in sand in our backyard, whipping cream in the kitchen, and permanent markers on the door.

My mom wasn't too happy with that last one. But hey, she told me I could try anything I could come up with to practice my spelling words.

My second grade teacher, Mrs. Halo, was the worst. She would red-flag my spelling test with an extra thick sharpie. It always looked like a war zone when I got it back.

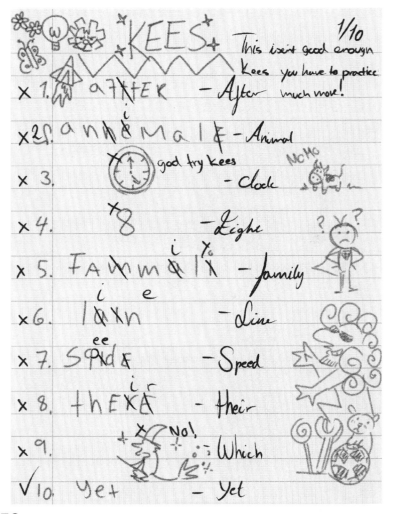

On top of the war zone, she also reprimanded me every time.

"Kees, I want you to write the word, not draw a picture. It's a *spelling* test not a *drawing* test! I have talked to you about this too often. You have to practice your words, you know that."

"Yes, I know, and I do practice a lot. A lot more than the other kids in class, that's for sure." I choked up and tears glistened in my eyes.

"It's just so hard. No matter how much time I put into it. It's not getting better."

"I think it's time to have you tested by the school psychologist, Kees." Mrs. Halo looked me in the eye. "Let's see if she can find out why you are having so much trouble."

So there I was, only a second grader, at the mercy of the school psychologist. She decided to test me on a few more things than just my trouble with spelling. A FEW more??? I felt like she squeezed me through the barrel in her office.

I don't know how many tests she did. I was there for hours and hours. On multiple days.

I had to listen to sentences and repeat them.

First, one small sentence of just a few words. Then, much longer sentences. Really hard. Another part of the test was that I had to recall a list of letters and numbers. She would give me random numbers and letters, and I had to put the letters in alphabetical order and numbers from low to high.

Like this one. She said 3 – A – 2. Then I had to put them in alphabetical and numeric order.

And the answer is... well, that's an easy one of course. The answer is 2 – 3 – A or A – 2 – 3.

I got those ok. After giving me the easy examples, it really started to get difficult.

1 – F – 4 – J
S – 7 – K – 2 – M
And it's not like I had all the time in the world for it. She wanted an answer right away. I

really sucked at these. While the psychologist was telling me the sequence, I had already forgotten it. It felt like being in a dark maze with all these numbers and letters coming at me and no way out.

After that, I had to read out loud. There is nothing I hate more. Then she asked me to spell words. Oh boy, here we go. However, there were also some really fun parts to this testing. Really. I probably liked it because it turns out I was really good at these.

Like, for example, the next one, where the figures inside the boxes form a pattern and I had to figure out which box in the answer row continues the pattern.

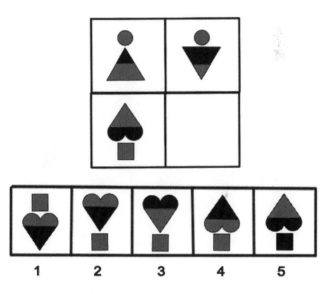

In 45 seconds or less!!!!

I killed it with those pattern questions. I saw the look on the school psychologist's face change from kind of tense to surprised.

She didn't say anything about it, though.

After all that hoopla was done, the school psychologist talked to my parents and teacher. What did they find from all those questions and tests?

I have a hard time with language. Reading, writing, spelling. No, REALLY??!?!?

But, here comes the best part. My test results in shapes and spaces were in the top of the WORLD. The top of the world!!!

That's when I found out what my superpower is.

The psychologist told my parents one other thing: I am dyslexic. Mom and Dad explained that it is a fancy word for having trouble with language. And I am not stupid after all. My IQ was just fine on the test.

I can't tell you how relieved I was about that. It was really bugging me big time that I am always the slowest in class and felt so stupid. I knew I wasn't stupid, but the fact that someone else, who really knows what she is talking about, tells me that I wasn't, was a real, real good message to hear.

Numbers don't lie. In this case, psychological test scores. In hindsight, I am actually glad they tested me. Finally, it all made sense. But that still doesn't change the fact that I have to take spelling tests, or write that essay.

11
NADMIL Grows

We need at least one more founding member for NADMIL. So the three of us decide to ask Meghan next. A girl, yes, but not a giggly, nail-polished barbie girl. We ask Meghan if she wants to be part of our secret group. She loves it.

"Give me some time to think about what I'm going to do for my application. You'll know soon enough when it's happening."

We don't have to wait long for Meghan's plan to unfold. This morning at the beginning of the school day, just when we all enter the classroom, we smell something really fishy. The Sticky Ticks gang start to gag, and I actually have to put my sweater over my nose and mouth. It is really, really bad. Imagine a mix of rotten eggs, fish, and bad breath.

Like bulls running out of a pen, we all rush through the door, eager to get fresh air. Mrs. Donow, who is trying to get in, is pushed back.

"Ho, ho, what's going on here?"

After assessing the damage, she decides that we aren't able to use our classroom anymore today. So we move around campus using different rooms that are free for an hour and have some super long recesses. We don't mind. Question was, who did it?

At first, everyone points at me. I am flattered.

This was a good joke, and I love to spend all the time I can get outside the classroom. But it wasn't me. Halfway through the day when no one has claimed the stink bomb, Meghan takes us aside.

"So... am I in?"

"Wait, it was you?"

"Shhh. Yes."

"Oh my, da bomb! Where did you get that

thing?" Pete asks.

"I'll tell you later, but it turned out great, don't you think?"

We all agree that Meghan has delivered us a better day at school with lots of recess time. And that's how NADMIL gets its fourth member.

12
Stupid

Days are long at Ladville Elementary School. And recess is waaaay too short. Every day it's the same routine, or almost the same. First read, write, and math before anything else. I don't understand why we can't switch things around, like have a science hour in the morning, or art class or another fun project.

But today our teacher makes us all really excited. "I have found such a fun project for today. We are going to make an actual crawling bug with a toothbrush and a battery."

"Huh?" Most kids look really puzzled.

I, on the other side, jump in the air.

"Yeah, can we start now!"

"After we finish our morning tasks in writing and math, Kees," the teacher replies. Of course, first the boring stuff, never the fun things first. But finally, after we arrive back from our lunch recess, there are toothbrushes and batteries everywhere.

"Cool, Pete! It's going to happen. I love it!"

"Kees, I want to be in your group." Pete pulls my arm.

"Of course, we are going to make the fastest bug of the class," I say, high fiving him.

"Kees! Time for your pull-out lesson."

Oh no, I forgot about that. That is the remedial teacher calling my name from the door opening. Ever since I found out I am dyslexic, I get pulled out of class a few times a week for some extra language lessons.

"Now? No, please, not now. We are about to make this cool bug."

I look at Mrs. Donow, my eyes begging like a Bambi that's about to be eaten by a gruesome wolf.

"I always get pulled out during science hour. It's not fair. Can I please stay this time? This time only?" I beg Mrs. Donow.

Pete is right behind me.

"Please, can Kees stay here for this project, for once?"

Mrs. Donow walks to the remedial teacher who is standing in the doorway waiting to collect me. They whisper and then the remedial teacher takes off.

"Kees, for this time only, you can stay and join the bug project."

"Yeah!" Pete and I high five again.

"Ok, let's start making groups," Mrs. Donow says.

Then, all of a sudden, I am popular. That never happens. Everyone wants to be in my group. Even the Sticky Ticks!

"Kees, can I be in your group?" the girls ask, smiling sweetly. "We really are helpless in these things, and you are so good at putting anything together."

Well, for once I agree with them. I don't even have to look at the instructions. I can see it in my head how to put the bug together.

"Bad luck, girls. Kees is going to be in my

group," Pete says with a smirk.

And that is that.

This afternoon makes a nice change from the usual morning routine.

The paragraph writing first thing. I hate that. All the other kids were penning away and my paper stayed white again.

After that, we read in our book. Oh boy, time to duck away again.

Stumbling over the simplest words makes me feel so stupid.

And I am NOT. I know for sure.

I know stupid from *feeling* stupid. You know who's brainless? Maria and her Sticky Tick girls.

This morning she proved herself again during math. The question was, "Would you rather have a large pizza in 6 slices or a large pizza in 9 slices?"

Her answer. Wait for it... "I would have the

large pizza in 6 slices because I can't eat the extra 3. That would be too much for me."

Really!

So I asked, "You really would rather have a large pizza in 6 slices instead of 9 slices? It's the same pizza, just divided in a different way."

They didn't get it.

"You don't get it."

"Oh, and how can our bright light be so sure," Sophie sneered.

"Because it's obvious, don't you see that?"

"How do you mean, 'obvious'? Not to us." Maria looked puzzled and annoyed.

"Ok, I can show you but then I want you to write my essay."

"We could, but the principal will probably notice that it's our text and not yours. If you know what I mean."

"Do you know what you want to write about?" Maria asked.

"No, not really."

"What is the hardest thing you've ever done?"
I asked the girls.

The girls had to think hard.

"Maybe math," said Sophie.

"Oh yeah, let me explain this pizza thing,
Maria and Sophie. Look here, we have two
pizzas. One divided in 6 slices and the other in 9
slices"

I drew it out on the board.

"No difference in size, do you agree?"

"Yes," Maria said, nodding. "Ah, now I see it. That's why you always draw so much, Kees. Now I understand. I guess we are better in writing and you are better in math and drawing."

That was probably one of the first nice things she ever said to me. I guess Maria isn't so stupid after all.

13
NADMIL Meetup

It's Saturday again, *hooray!*, and time for a
NADMIL meeting at our base, the shed in my
backyard. Tom brings cookies (he's such a
cookie monster), and I bring a pint of vanilla ice
cream with four spoons.

"With this, I call our NADMIL meeting open!" I say while hitting the spoon against the ice cream carton.

"Pete and I got into a little bit of trouble last Wednesday, as you might know," I say.

We then share our remote control prank with Tom and Meghan.

"Pete, did you get your essay done?" I ask.

"Not yet, but I know what I'm going to do, I think," Pete replies. "I'll probably write it tomorrow."

"About what?" We all look at Pete.

"I think I'm going to write about the club soccer tryouts. That was so hard because I was very nervous."

"And you, Kees?" asks Meghan.

"I have no idea. Do any one of you have a suggestion? I have been racking my brain."

"What about that robotic contest you did? Wasn't that the hardest thing you ever did?" Meghan says helpfully.

98

"Nah, that was fun and easy peasy."

"Or the Lego city you built for the holiday display at City Hall?" Tom mentions.

"That was a lot of work, but not difficult."

"Ok, what else?" Tom is getting impatient.

"I don't know yet. It'll come to me. I hope. Let's move on with our meeting."

We talk about what we are going to do this week and finish the pint of ice cream and cookies.

Oh, and Tom farts so badly that he smokes us all out of the shed.

"Man, what did you eat? You are rotten inside, wafting like a buffalo on a hot summer day!" I say, holding my nose.

Time to wrap it up.

I head back to the kitchen and decide that I finally am going to try and write something, just anything, to get a start on this stupid essay. Just when I am ready with my piece of paper, twirling my pencil around on it, Bobby enters. He is reading a book while walking and does not even notice me at first.

"Ugh," I sigh.

Bobby looks up from his book.

"What are you doing? This is very rare to see you with a notebook in front of you."

"I have to write that essay, remember."

"Ah, yeah. Are you still not done with that?"

"Don't look so surprised. You know this is hard for me. And no. I haven't even started. I really have no clue what to write or how for that matter."

"Well, does it really matter what you write. I would just slap something down. Who is going to read it anyway?" Bobby laughs.

"If I even could do that, just *slap* something down. You are talking like it's just so easy."

"Well, yeah, isn't it? You can write about anything you like, so just let your imagination go wild. I would not even need a half hour to get two pages full."

"Of course. Gah!" I clamp my fingers around my pencil and almost break it in two. Of course he would only need just half an hour.

"I can let my imagination go wild, but only in my head. Not on paper!" I hiss.

"Well, I can't help you then." Bobby sighs.

He grabs a drink out of the fridge and off he goes. Leaving me with my blank piece of paper. What a mess.

14
Grandpa

Sunday is family day at our house. This means my parents take me and my little brother to visit our uncle and aunt or Grandpa and Grandma.

Today we are going to see our grandpa and grandma, or Opa and Oma to me.

"Hey, Keesmans!" My grandpa is always happy to see me. "Come sit on my lap, and I'll tell you a story. Grandma shouldn't hear this, so *shhhh*."

Oh, please don't tell anyone I am still sitting on Opa's lap. I don't want that going around. I just really enjoy it. He is such a cuddle bear, that Opa of mine.

"How is my favorite grandson doing? Did you do something fun lately?"

Well, of course I did. I tell Opa the whole story of the remote control escapade. Grandpa slaps his knee, laughing.

"That's my boy; very good, Kees."

"So, Opa, what's the hardest thing you ever did? I need to come up with something for my essay, so maybe you can give me some ideas?"

"The hardest thing I ever did?" Opa frowns and mumbles. "Let me think. Oh, yes. Are you ready for this?" he whispers in my ear. "The hardest thing I ever did was telling your grandma to stop spending money! It's like her wallet is burning a hole in her pocket," he says, with a big grin from ear to ear.

"Really, Opa? That doesn't sound too hard to me."

"Have you ever said 'no' to Oma? I did once, and she stopped talking to me, she refused to do anything in the house and didn't go grocery shopping for weeks. Oma was on strike, and I got the silent treatment."

"That doesn't sound nice, but was that really the hardest thing you ever did?"

"Ah, I guess not, just kidding around with you a little, Kees. But you do have to be careful what you wish for with Oma. She can be a tough cookie."

Right at that moment Oma walks in with a tray of cookies.

"Yes, Oma, just what we needed," Opa says, grabbing a handful.

"Oma, what is the hardest thing you ever did?"

"Marrying that cookie monster you are sitting

on!" she says as she taps Opa on his fingers.

"Or maybe it was the stupidest thing I ever did," Oma snorts as she walks outside where the rest of the family is.

"Ok, Opa, help me here. I need to write this thing before Wednesday, and I don't have a clue what to do."

"What was difficult for you, Kees? Moving to another town? Making new friends?"

"Not really. Surprisingly, that went pretty smoothly."

"What about that Lego building business you set up last summer?"

"That's fun, Opa, and really easy for me."

"Living under one roof with your little brother? I know you fight a lot."

"Hmm, maybe, he is so annoying. Always me, me, me and the first with everything! The first to be able to tie his shoes, the first to be able to write his name, the first ready with his homework – always – yadda, yadda, yadda. He's really annoying sometimes. How do I write about that? I don't want to give him the pedestal of being the first in everything! He likes to be the center of attention. Not on my watch; that's not going to happen!"

"Why is my little boy curled up like a gremlin on my lap? What's going on, Kees? You look like you're feeling down?"

"I just can't write anything, Opa. It's so hard for me!"

"Well, there you have it, Kees! You just answered your own question. I know how you feel, love. Your Opa really doesn't like to write or read for that matter, either. I remember feeling overwhelmed at school when I was little. When it was summer, I was cheerful and happy. By the time it was fall, that cheerfulness was gone.

Summer   FAll   Winter   Spring

In winter, I started to get stomach aches at school, and my mom had to pick me up early several times. By the time it was spring, I was scraping my nose on the concrete. That's how bent over I felt from the constant failure I was feeling.

I was so tired of trying, of putting more effort into school than everyone else and still falling further and further behind."

"Yes, yes," I say, nodding. "You know, I feel the same way, Opa."

"But you know what, Kees? All of that will change when you get older and you get to do the things you are really good at. Opa always knew how to fix things. One of my summer jobs when I was a teenager was helping out my uncle. He had a store with washing machines, refrigerators, that kind of stuff. I helped him with repairs, and soon enough I was so good at it, that he let me go fix fridges at the clients' houses on my own. That's where I started working after I finished school. I ended up taking over his business when he retired and built it out to a whole chain of stores and repair services.

"So, you see, Kees. There's a whole world out there with thousands of jobs and things to do that don't require a lot of writing. **Ideas are what's important, not the ability to write a sequence of letters.**

"No one ever invented or discovered something like the telephone or electricity because they knew how to spell perfectly. And I know you are bursting with ideas. You will get there. But yes, you first have to go through school and learn the basics. You cannot do without it. So buck up, my boy!

"Straighten your back, chin up! Come on, Opa can't straighten his back anymore, but you can. Say this after me and fill in the end. Grandpa does the first one. Listen carefully!

"I AM GOOD AT... TALKING.

"How about you, Kees, finish the sentence I AM GOOD AT..."

I repeat, "I AM GOOD AT... Legos!"

"I AM GOOD AT... fixing things!"

"I AM GOOD AT... drawing!"

"I AM GOOD AT... making friends!"

"Yes, Kees," Grandpa says, waving with his arms. "Go on!"

"I AM GOOD AT... building!"

"I AM GOOD AT... NADMIL!"

"I AM GOOD AT... making fun!"

In the end, we are both chanting and high fiving.

"I AM GOOD AT... helping others!"

Opa gives me a big hug.

"Thank you, Opa. It always helps when I talk to you."

"I told you I am good at talking; Opa knows his stuff."

15
D-Day

Before you know it, it's Wednesday again, and for me and Pete, it is D-Day.

On our way to school, Pete asks me what I am dreading. "Were you able to get something down after looking at it together the other day?"

"No," I mumble. "I also got some help offered from Mrs. Donow and even Maria, but it didn't help."

"What, Maria? Is there something brewing between the two of you?"

"Pete, come on. Never!"

"I'm not sure about that?" Pete teases.

"Are you keeping something a secret from your best friend?"

"Oh, stop it, Pete, you know I would never in

a million years fall for someone like Maria!

"What about you, Pete?" I say, taking the attention off me. "Are you done with your essay?"

"Yeah, I jotted something down real quick last night." Pete holds up the paper. "But I won't

hand it in if you don't, either!"

"You have to hand it in, Pete. I don't want you to sit in for recess. Who knows, it might take me weeks to get it done. I don't want to drag you into this."

"Are you sure, Kees?"

"Yes, absolutely."

During the first recess, we go to Mr. Lamares' office to hand in our essays. Another recess out the door.

"So, gentlemen," he says.

"I hope you enjoyed this assignment and thought about your actions that caused this?"

Pete hands over his essay.

"This was actually a lot better than trash duty."

Ugh, well, not for me. I will do trash duty 100 times over this senseless essay. I have been sitting at my desk the last two days after school for several hours with nothing to show for it. Well, I've got one sentence on paper. But that's it!

"I am sorry, I don't have anything, Mr. Lamares."

"How come, Kees?"

"It just isn't easy for me to write. That's kind of the problem, because that's what the essay was going to be about."

"Well, you know the consequences. Maybe your teacher can help you while you stay in for recess to finish your task?"

Darn, I was hoping to skip the essay and do something else. It doesn't look that way. I guess I'm stuck for the time being.

"I hope you both think twice before you add any more shenanigans to your school record."

I guess we won't be able to do any more pranks because we're almost done with elementary school. Finally.

So here I am, my worst nightmare coming true. I cannot go out for recess, and I have to write two pages. While my classmates are running out of the classroom, I am stuck at my desk.

Mrs. Donow is really not happy either because she has to stay in with me. She offers me some of her lemonade to sweeten the sour situation.

"What can I do to help you, Kees?"

"I don't know. It's not really that I don't know what to write about. It's all in my head. Getting it on paper is the challenge."

Then the ear-piercing fire alarm stops us in our tracks.

"What is this? Come on, Kees, we have to leave the classroom and do our emergency drill." Mrs. Donow grabs her safety backpack and helmet.

"I am sure it's a false alarm, but you never know. So let's start with our safety drill."

Mrs. Donow walks to the center of the schoolyard and gathers her class at the designated spot. I follow and see Pete, Tom, and Meghan with a grin from ear to ear. Ah ha! Wait, is this a NADMIL operation?

"Guys," I whisper. "Is this what I think it is?"

All three nod and put their thumbs up.

"We saved you, shhhhh... Don't tell anyone," says Pete.

Well, of course not. This is pretty rad.

"We will tell you later how we did it, but we thought you could use a bit of a breather."

"Yeah, you could say that. This is awesome, guys."

NADMIL proves its value. Real friends.

The next half hour we have to stay in our designated spot while the principal figures out what the alarm is all about.

I have three packets of chewing gum in my pocket. I always like to chew gum when I need to do something I'm not good at. So I took a big stack from home since I knew I had to perform today.

"How many pieces of gum can you chew at once?" Tom asks, grinning. "Let's do a little game."

Tom starts counting, putting one, two, three,

four big pieces in his mouth. Chewing slower and slower with every next piece. Five and six.

That is about it for Tom.

Pete and Meghan can only fit four.

I try to break Tom's record, but I know he has a big mouth. For real. So I kind of give up at five. My jaws are hurting. Ouch.

Tom takes the wad of gum out of his mouth and pulls it apart like an elastic band.

"Shhhh," Tom whispers. "How many times do you think this fits around Charlie's head?"

Charlie is sitting right behind him with his

back towards Tom.

"Is this a bet?" I ask.

"Yes, why not?"

"Ok, Charlie has a humongous head of hair, so I think about four times."

"Meghan?"

"Probably six times."

"Pete?"

"Ten times for sure."

Tom stands up, and with lightning speed throws a loop of bubble gum over Charlie's head

and starts winding the next loop.

"Whoa!" Charlie ducks down and throws his hands in the air, trying to fend off Tom and the chewing gum.

"What on earth are you doing?"

By now, it is too late for Charlie. Tom has looped two strings of bubble gum around his head and his hair is one gooey, sticky mess.

The little riot catches the attention of Mrs. Donow.

"What's going on here?"

"Oh, nothing special."

We all smile and stand in a circle around Charlie.

"Kids, the alarm is cleared and we can go back to our room."

"Can we go to the bathroom first?" Tom asks.

"Yes, I will see you back in class in a few minutes."

"Come on, Charlie, let's go," I urge him.

Tom, Pete, Charlie, and I run to the boys' bathroom. Charlie looks in the mirror and touches the gum.

"Guys, what the heck?"

We all try to pull the bright pink bubble gum from his long, curly blond hair. It looks as if he has a sweatband on.

"This gum is not coming out anytime soon, I'm afraid."

"Here's my cap, Charlie. Put it on and we will figure out what to do later." Pete is always on top of things.

"My hair is ruined. I will never be able to get this sticky mess out. You are all going to pay for this, big time!"

"Ok, ok, let's go to class and we'll talk about it after school," I say, trying to sound reassuring.

Right after school, Charlie is waiting for us at the gate.

"You better have a plan because you don't want to meet my dad OR mom for that matter."

Charlie's dad is a tall, strong firefighter and his mom is a hairdresser. She will probably flip if she sees Charlie with so much bubble gum in his hair.

"Let's go to the NADMIL shed and we will give you a first-class hair treatment," I suggest.

"To what?" Charlie frowns.

On the way to the shed, we explain to Charlie what NADMIL is and invite him to become a member. After all, he did act pretty cool when we threw him this curveball.

In the shed, we google how to get bubblegum out of hair.

This is what it says:

1. Find a jar of creamy peanut butter or vegetable oil, such as olive oil.
2. Cover the gum completely with peanut butter or oil using your fingers or an old toothbrush.
3. Wait a few minutes to allow the oil to work.
4. Remove the gum from the hair.

I go inside our house to find all of the items
we need for the operation and come back with
the peanut butter, olive oil, old toothbrushes, a
comb, towels, and two pints of ice cream with
spoons.

"Welcome to hair salon 'pink bubble,'" I crow.
Charlie sits down on a crate. We cover his
shoulders with a towel and start spreading the
peanut butter and olive oil on his hair. One thing
leads to another and before we know it, we are
in a peanut butter smack-fest.

When every speck of gum in his hair is covered in oil, we take a break and eat our ice cream.

The entire shed, our hands, our clothes, everything smells like a mixture of peanut butter and olive oil. Quite an interesting combination, I must say. We are covered in it, too.

During our break, we fill Charlie in on a few NADMIL essentials. He does have to apply, of course, but we are going to be easy on him. Staying cool as a cucumber while bubble gum is thrown in your hair is actually already pretty impressive.

Luckily, the gum comes out pretty easily.

"I'll have my mom fix the rest in her salon."

Charlie is unfazed, even though he smells like an olive tree with peanuts, and his hair falls slick around his head like a wet '70s hippy.

I wish I could be so easygoing. That would make my life a lot easier. I will have to try and learn how Charlie does it. Good thing he is going to be in NADMIL.

"Let's try to determine if Charlie has an Apple or Android brain." Meghan is always very practical, and since we all did the what-kind-of-brain-you-have quiz, we might as well check Charlie.

"Wait, what?" For Charlie, we are speaking in NADMIL code. "I have no clue what you're all talking about."

"You will figure it out soon enough. Just do what we ask, and your answers will give us an idea of the nuts and bolts of your brain," Meghan explains.

"Does it hurt?" Charlie says, jittery.

"Give me the list, Tom."

Tom yanks a little piece of paper from a nail and gives it to me.

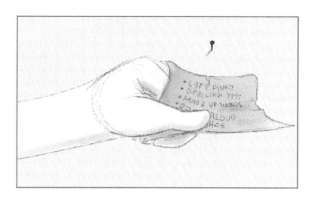

"Ok, Charlie, point your left pinky to the right of your nose."

Charlie starts lifting his right hand up and halfway switches to his left.

"Oops, wrong side." After the false start, he does point his left pinky on the right side of his nose.

I have to check my socks for this one.

"You are using your sock trick, I see it, Kees!" Meghan points at my rocket sock on my right.

"What trick?" Charlie asks, curious.

"Kees always wears socks that can tell him what's left and right. Look!"

They all look at my socks.

"Left with lollipops and right with rockets,"

Meghan points out.

Charlie smiles.

"I could use that. Smart."

"Ok, let's continue. Next up. Take this piece of paper. We're going to do a spelling test."

"What? Why?" Charlie frowns. "Can't we do something else? Something I am better at? I suck at spelling."

"What are you better at then, Charlie?"

"Well, drawing the word instead of writing it, for example."

"Ok, great. We know enough."

"On to the next thing."

"So I don't have to do the spelling test?" Charlie asks.

"Nope, you already gave us the answer we needed."

"Huh?"

Meghan took a book out of her bag. "Read this page aloud."

"Oh, no," Charlie sighs. "Another of my not-so-favorite things to do! Why don't you ask me about my favorite things instead?"

"Ok, let's hear it, Charlie. Go ahead. Your favorite things."

"Let me think." Charlie frowns. He takes his time.

"Ok, got it. I am going to sing it like 'the favorite things' song from *The Sound of Music.* Ok?"

"Sounds good to us."

"Here we go...

🎵 🎵 *drumming and singing and riddles and*

motors.

> *Acting real scary and fixing some rotors.*
>
> *Race cars and painting a wall full of wings.*
>
> *These are a few of my favorite things!"*

"You just made that up, Charlie? Cool," I say.
"Now for something completely different: When
was the first time you tied your shoe laces all
by yourself? Without the help of your mom or
anyone else?"

"Uh, why do you need to know that? What a weird question, you guys."

"Just answer it, Charlie. Don't keep asking! We know what we're doing."

"You know, my mom always bought me shoes with Velcro until last year. So I don't really know. Last year I guess?"

"You never had shoe laces?"

"I did, but I never wanted to use those shoes because it took me way too long to tie my laces."

"Oh, man, you tick all the boxes."

"What boxes?"

"Of the Apple brain. Am I thinking what you're thinking, Meghan and Pete?"

"Yes, we have another Apple brain in NADMIL. Perfect. Two Android and three Apple brains."

"Ok, Charlie," I say. "Let me ask you one more thing. Maybe you remember, maybe not. When I was little, I made up my own words. Like 'schabetti' for spaghetti and 'mawn lower.' Do you have any of those for us to share?"

"Let me think... Ha, yes, I really do! I always said 'hamgaberg' and 'aminal.' I still do actually."

"Yep, you are an Apple, Charlie!" I cheer.

"Welcome to NADMIL!"

16
Speech to Text

The next day, I am back at the drawing board, or rather at the writing desk in class.

"Kees, maybe you can use one of those speech-to-text apps to get your story on paper?"

This is actually a very good idea from Mrs. Donow. After all, I am allowed to type my essay instead of hand-write it. Normally, we are not allowed to use the computer or apps for writing because we could use spell check and copy and paste things. So stupid! It would make things so much easier for me at school. As if we are going to write anything handwritten later in life at college or in a job. I don't understand why the school is so strict about it.

"Can I install the app on one of the school computers?"

There, I open another big can of worms. Of course a student cannot install something on a classroom computer. It has to be approved by the principal and the tech guy. That could take another few days. If it is allowed at all!

"You know what, Mrs. Donow, I will do it at home tonight on my computer."

Tonight, I sit down in front of my computer and ramble in one stretch. Why didn't I think of doing this earlier?

It isn't perfect and it wasn't done in one go, but at least I got it started.

The next day during recess, Mrs. Donow helps me and I correct and change the things I added the night before. I am getting somewhere. In just two days, I am almost done – two whole pages written. It is a miracle, to say the least.

I gave it to my mom to read that night. About ten minutes later she called me in.

She had tears in her eyes. Oh no!

"Is it that bad, Mom?!"

"No, silly," she cried and smiled at the same time. "This is really, really good, Kees. I am super impressed. Come give me a big hug. I am so proud of you."

Wow, that's nice for a change. What a great feeling. Slam dunk!

17
The Actual Essay

The hardest thing I ever did.

Mr. Lamares! You asked me to write about the hardest thing I ever did. At first I didn't know what that would be for me. I racked my brain and had to think for a long time. I also got the "voluntary" advice from my parents, teacher, some friends and eventually my grandpa. When I talked to him, it all became very clear.

You said being a principal is a very difficult job. That can be the case, but you _chose_ to be a principal. If you don't like it, you can walk away from it and do something else. At least I would!

The hardest thing I ever did is not something I can walk away from. It's there every day, day in, day out, and will never go away.

To understand what that means for me, I am going to ask you to solve this little puzzle.

You can use this key to read the line below it:

```
a=z b=y c=x d=w e=v f=u g=t h=s
i=r j=q k=p l=o m=n n=m o=l p=k
g=j r=i s=h t=g u=f v=e w=d x=c
y=b z=a
```

Gsv sziwvhg gsrmt uli nv vevi zmw zodzbh droo yv gl ivzw, dirgv zmw hkvoo.

Do you know what it says? Did you solve the puzzle?

Tiring right? Frustrating maybe? Is it irritating?

A whole new language for you? Imagine having to use this key for every single word, sentence, and paragraph you read every day. Everywhere. At school, at home, downtown.

This is what it feels like for me to read and write. I am hacking code on a daily basis.

This means I am the slowest reader in class. Always the last to finish, as you maybe now can imagine after doing just that one little sentence. Spelling is a disaster for me too, and writing will always be a challenge. This makes me feel stupid and frustrated and tired.

And you know, I am actually good at a lot of things. Like coming up with fun spoofs, fixing things, drawing, figuring out how things work, Legos and such. My grandpa said: *"Ideas are what's important, not the ability to write a string of letters."* I so agree.

I know that we need to learn to read and write at school. And I found out I can write great things. Look at what you're reading right now. I didn't think I could do it when you gave me this punishment.

I can do it, but I really, really need extra time to work on assignments, and I need more practice and more help from the teacher and spellcheck. I am sure that is the same for all code hackers at school. I know a few.

Mrs. Donow told me she sometimes wonders how I came up with the ideas for the funny, weird, or special story I wrote. I figured out I can write like my classmates if I get the extra time and help. That would make school so much better for me. I feel so much more motivated, happier, and more confident than I was for a long time at school, just because I wrote this all down for you.

Mr. Lamares, you told me your job is sometimes difficult. It can't be as hard as hacking the code day in and day out. Can you do something for us code hackers?

For me it's too late because I am almost out of elementary school. But for all the other code hackers, you could make their lives so much better. You would be the hero that made it all happen!

DONE!!!!!!!!!

The next school day, I hand in my essay and I am free at last. What a relief! I can't tell you how this weighed down on me. It's over, done, *finito*, finished, slam-dunk!!!

Yeah! Recess time!

18
Awards Season

It's Friday, and elementary school is almost over for me. Just one more week. I am counting the days. I won't be missing the good, the more often bad, and the occasional pile of ugly of school. Summer, I am ready!

Mom is nagging me at breakfast.

"I want you to wear that dress shirt I bought for you the other week to school today. The white one with the little black dots."

"A dress shirt? Why? I never wear a dress shirt to school."

"Today you should. As a mom, I am sometimes allowed to give you instructions on how to dress. So today, that's what you are wearing."

"But why?"

"Kees!" Mom is looking at me as if she is going to unplug the WiFi for the entire summer. Meanwhile Bobby walks down the stairs in his Sunday shirt.

"You, too?" I frown.

"Yeah, Mom said to wear this," Bobby says, walking proudly past me.

"Okaaayyyy. I will wear it."

"I just ironed it; it's hanging on your door handle," Mom yells.

So I leave home, dressed up, feeling like a penguin. When Pete sees me, he has to laugh.

"Why are you walking so stiff?"

"It's this shirt, man. It makes me feel that way."

"Nice shirt, by the way. What's the occasion?"

"Mom wanted me to wear it. She insisted!"

"Ah, actually my mom said the same, but I totally forgot about it."

Why are our moms all of a sudden so concerned about what we wear to school?

When we arrive at school, the mystery is solved: it's assembly this morning. Totally forgot about that. And there are more kids wearing things they normally only would wear at Easter brunch. Mom, why me???

We go to our classroom first. Mrs. Donow quickly starts the day with the flag.

After that is done, we head over to the auditorium where the entire school pours in.

It's a tight squeeze, and as fifth graders, we are allowed to sit on the back benches behind all the little kids sitting cross-legged on the floor. There is some justice after all.

And now it dawns on me. It's awards season. That's why some kids are dressed up, and I also see some parents in the back. Or actually, I only see cameras, lots of them.

Why on earth did my mom tell me to dress up? I have never won an award. Ever. Pete has, and Meghan also. I suspect the usual bunch will get awards again. What's new? It's always soooo boring. I hate it. It takes for.ev.er! Did I mention that? Certainly when you don't feel part of it.

After singing the school song, Mr. Lamares walks up to the front and starts his speech.

"Dear students, teachers, and parents, welcome to the Ladville Elementary end-of-the-year awards ceremony. Today, I feel very privileged and honored to stand here in front of you all and acknowledge the achievements of our brilliant students who have made both the school and their parents proud.

Awards are a way to encourage good behavior and positive competitive spirit. A way for me as principal, and the teachers, to recognize student achievement. So, today we are giving away the awards in mainly five categories: academics, attendance, behavior, character, and extra curricular."

OMG, this is going to last for.ev.er! I already feel uncomfortable on the hard bench, and we haven't even started.

The principal goes on.

"Before we start, I would like to thank our teachers for taking our school to new heights and creating a wonderful environment for our students to flourish. I would also like to thank all the parents for joining us and making this occasion a huge success. Thank you!

So here we go, kids, bear with me. We are going to do this as streamlined as possible. I am asking you to hold your applause for every individual award winner and wait until I have finished the category. Then we can all cheer for the winners at once."

"In the academics category, we have the following award winners..."

Well, I don't have to be afraid to be called up for this one. In fact, I have never received an award. A school award that is. I did get an award

for soccer once.

But then again, everyone received an award with soccer. It's a super ugly statue, by the way.

"The awards for the super reader go to Maria and Bobby." What? I am flabbergasted. Bobby wins an award, stickler!

"Come up, Maria and Bobby! Hold your applause, please."

Maria's parents are already clapping but realize they shouldn't when everyone looks at them. An awkward smile follows. They are beaming with pride, of course. Oh, how I hate these awards ceremonies.

I see Charlie's parents and wave at them. What catches my eye... Mom?

What is she doing here? I think this is the first time she's ever been to our awards ceremony. Ah, of course, she got an invitation because Bobble got an award. Duh!

The principal continues.

"Our super scientist award this year goes to Ryan." Ryan screams.

Followed by: most improved student, math facts hero, multiplier whiz, and so on and so on. Pete gets the multiplier whiz, by the way. High five for him!

Finally applause. On to the next category.

"Character awards," Mr. Lamares continues.

The trustworthiness award goes to Jake, citizenship to Maura, responsibility award, kindness is for Vera and so on. And again applause.

Are we done yet?

Behavior awards.

I sure am not a candidate for one of those.

"The positivity award goes to Charlie."

Wow, man, I knew it. He is always so positive. Charlie waves to his parents while he walks up to the front of the auditorium, swerving past third graders and teeny first graders.

In the meantime, the volunteer, citizenship, leadership, and helpfulness awards recipients are called up.

Applause.

The perfect attendance award goes to Sam. Well, yeah, Sam got us all sick this year because he came to school while he had the flu. That made the rest of us sick: even the teacher had to stay home sick for a few days.

The extracurricular awards.

Maybe there is a tiny chance I get one? The music award, afterschool star, and hall hero monitor awards (the one that keeps the hallway safe from bullies) go to Sophie. That is a surprise to me. I never knew she did all that. Good for her.

And a few more awards. Again, applause, although it is fading off pretty fast. We are all kinda done.

"This is almost the conclusion of our awards ceremony." The principal smiles.

Fantastic, finally! Everyone starts to move. The principal waves his arms. The teachers hold up the quiet sign.

"Whoa, whoa, whoa," Mr. Lamares interrupts, "stay seated."

"I said ALMOST done! I have one more very special award to hand out."

The principal tries not to raise his voice. Everyone sits down again, disappointed.

"I have personally created this next award for a student who opened my eyes this year. Unexpectedly, I received a special assignment from this student suggesting that we look at the ways of teaching to each individual student, especially the ones who are hacking code every day. It's important that we value and celebrate the strengths of every student. Whether they are good in math, English, art, sports, science, or music. Everyone is different.

Because of this student's fresh take on our school, I am going to change a few things, starting next school year.

But first, I want to award this student the new and honorable Most Valuable Student (MVS) award, which also comes with one free pizza per week for a full year!

"This MVS award goes to...... Kees!"

What!?!?!

Everybody stands up and starts clapping.

Holy cow. Did the principal just call my name?

I look back at my mom who is in tears. Giving me a heart sign.

"Go, Kees!" Pete pushes me towards the front. I stumble through the crowd. I can't believe it. MVS. Never saw that one coming.

The principal hands me the award and a pizza box.

"Thank you, Kees. It wasn't always easy being

your principal, but I sure will never forget your

pranks and your essay. It opened my eyes."

19
Summer!

One week later and it's summer! Freedom, sleepovers, camping, doodling, freewheeling, and NADMIL. Oh, and a free pizza every week!

All NADMIL members come to my shed for our first summer meeting.

"So, Kees, are we going to have pizza at our meetings this year?" Tom smiles.

Pete is in favor.

"Yeah, what a surprise, huh? I was totally caught off guard by our principal."

"Not our principal anymore," Charlie reminds us.

"You're right. I finally earned some credit with him, and now I can't use it because we are done!"

"What did you write to him, Kees? It must have impressed him a ton." Meghan looks curious.

"Oh, nothing special. Just that they should give us Apple brains the extra time and possibility to get good grades and shine just like the kids with Android brains. If you know what I mean."

"Not really, Kees?" Meghan and Pete are looking clueless.

"Well, you know, almost everyone in school – teachers, principal, and most kids – have an Android brain. So, the teacher explains something in 'Android' code, and the kids receive it in their brain, and it makes sense. But if you have an Apple brain, that Android code the teacher is sending out isn't translated one-on-one in that Apple brain."

"Just like you can't run Android software on an Apple device. I am constantly hacking the Android code to make something of it, if anything. I explained that to Mr. Lamares. The school needs to give lessons to those kids with an Apple brain in the right code. Simple!"

Pete is in deep thought. You can see his head making overtime. "So, that would help you in school, Kees?"

"Yes, I think so. But hey, I'm not in elementary anymore, so I won't get that help."

Pete is still churning.

"You are so much better at the things I have a hard time with. Like figuring out how to put a project together, like the bugs, remember?"

"Yeah, and you are so much better than me in writing up the report after a project." I wink at Pete.

"We're just a good team. We will get a lot further together than alone. Look at NADMIL. Apple and Android brains united." Meghan starts a high five.

"How would anyone know what code works best for them, by the way?" Pete asks.

"Our NADMIL test, of course." Charlie jumps

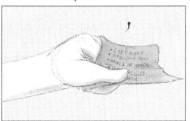

up and plucks the questions from the nail on the wall.

"Let's sell the test this summer. We can make big bucks!!!!"

"No, no. No one should know about our group, Charlie. That would ruin it. Besides, the test is sooo not scientifically proven. Ha, ha. They should ask an adult to look into it. Get them tested like my over-the-top test by the school psychologist. Nothing scary about that."

"Back to summer, my NADMIL friends. What are our plans? NADMILLERS??? Hellooooo???"

They all start screaming at each other.

"Go to the pool!"

"Camping!"

"Woodworking camp!"

"Eat lots and lots of pizza! And ice cream!"

"We are just going to have the best summer EVER!!!"

164

"Summer!!!"

How about you?

Hey, you!

Yes, I am talking to you! What kind of brain do you have?

Do you think you have an Apple brain just like me? Do you recognize some of the things in my experience at school, with homework – or spelling???

If so, then take this book to an adult and talk to them about it.

And you know what else? I would love to see your stories about **YOU** Hacking the Code, by tagging your pictures, story, or video with **#hackingthecode**.

Psssst! If you dare, also tag your secret friends group posts.

Try These Test Questions

Your turn. Do you want to try the test questions I had to do with the psychologist?

Ask someone to read the sequences on the next page (don't look just yet!!!) and repeat them in alphabetical order and the numbers from low to high.

Don't look. Really??? If you really want to try and feel the same way I felt, you shouldn't look at it beforehand.

Hi, stranger. You are going to test this newbie's skills. Read these mixed-up sequences of letters and numbers one by one and have them repeat back in alphabetical order for the letters and the numbers from low to high.[1]

Like this one:

E – B – 6   answer: 6 – B – E or B- E – 6

Ok, here we go. Ready?

8 – 2 – P   answer: 2 – 8 – P or P – 2 – 8

3 – Z – 5 – K

answer: 3 – 5 – K – Z or K – Z – 3 – 5

5 – U – 7 – H – 9

answer: 5 – 7 – 9 – H – U or H – U – 5 – 7 – 9

1   Source: WISC-V Wechsler intelligence scale for children – Fifth edition record form and response booklet 1.

N – 6 – B – 2 – C – 1 – T – 3

answer: 1 – 2 – 3 – 6 – B – C – N – T

And the last and longest one:

2 – P – 7 – K – 4 – B – 8 – Z

answer: 2 – 4 – 7 – 8 – B – K – P – Z

And how did it go?

It's impossible, right? Certainly those last ones. At least for me it was. I guess I didn't score well on those at all. If you did well, which of course can be the case, you probably have an Android brain.

They tend to do better on these sorts of tasks (or so I have been told).

However, there were also some really fun parts to this testing. Really. I probably liked it because it turns out I was really good at these.

Like, for example, this one where the figures inside the boxes form a pattern, and I had to figure out which box in the answer row continues the pattern.

Try them.

Test question 1:

Look at the five symbols in the top box.

Which of the symbols in the bottom row continue

the pattern?

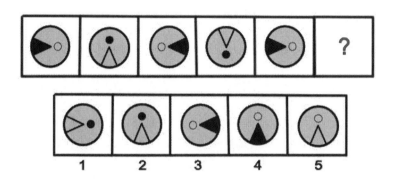

In 45 seconds or less!!!!

Want to know the answer to this example?
It's at the end of these test questions.

Did you solve it? Within 45 seconds? How did
your mom, dad, or friend do? Ask them.

Test question 2:

Look at the three symbols in the top box.
Which of the symbols in the bottom row continue
the pattern?

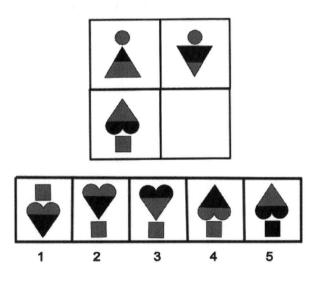

Test question 3:

Which of these figures in the boxes (1 through 5) weighs the same as the star on the left of the question mark?

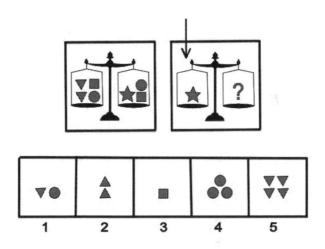

Test question 4:

Which of these figures in the boxes (1 through 5) weighs the same as the symbols on the scale next to the question mark?

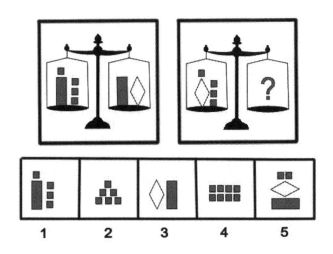

Next one. Are you with me?

I had to do these kinds of tasks for hours at a stretch with no slack time. So, *you* can't take a break between questions, either.

Test question 5:

Fill in the question mark with one of the items from the boxes below. A chicken is to an egg like a cow is to?

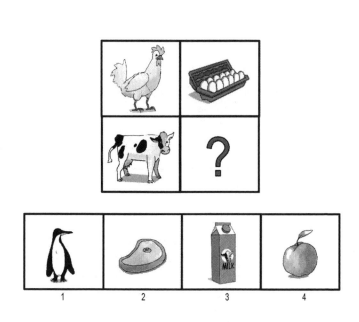

And the last one.

Test question 6:

Choose a picture from each row that goes together. Why?

And???

How did it go?

Were you able to do them? If you are good at these, then you probably have more of an Apple brain, just like me. But I'm not a psychologist, so if you want to be sure, you should do a fun (*ahem*) real test.

The answers to the picture questions are:

Question 1: answer – 2

Question 2: answer – 2

Question 3: answer – 2

Question 4: answer – 4

Question 5: answer – 3

Question 6: answer – 2, 5, 9 (these items all hold something together)[2]

Acknowledgements

It takes a village to raise a kid, and a world of villagers, spread all over the globe, to create this book. It is with enormous gratitude that I would like to thank everyone involved, one way or another. Thank you Nils, and my family, for allowing me to write this story, with some of the experiences we lived through as an example.

I could not have done this without the expertise in illustration and insight into dyslexia of Mads Johan Øgaard. The moment he read the manuscript he was 'in'. Thank you, Mads, for being a pillar of support and such a pleasure to work with.

Thank you, Anne Marie Nietsch, for the wise lessons in our coaching sessions. Thank you, Anne Gillelan and Mary Jo Winefordner, for your support and reading the very early versions of the manuscript. Thank you to proofreaders Liv (9), Mariah Holliday, Nikki Romano, and Robert Rabinowitz. Lisa Davis brought the manuscript to the next level with her developmental edit and Jennifer Rees with a finishing edit. A special thanks to Belen Guillen and her son Oliver (8) for beta reading, and introducing the manuscript to his teacher, Mrs. Hart, and her entire third grade class. Thank you, Meike van de Ven, for your cover design input. It has been a really fun ride, and a great learning experience.

NEVER A DULL MOMENT

About

Author

Gea Meijering is a creative writer, seasoned marketeer, parent mentor, and artist with a passion and a mission. As the mother of a dyslexic son, she researched dyslexia better than an FBI agent would, and witnessed the dyslexia struggle and gift it can be, upfront and personal. Gea volunteered as a parent mentor for the special education department of her local school district and is a dynamic dyslexia

advocate.

Over the years she saw many kids and their parents struggling to find out why school wasn't going well. Reason to write a children's book that offers kids and families the opportunity to identify with the different characters, make visible the learning struggles some students go through, and bring dyslexia awareness to the community.

Illustrator

Mads Johan Øgaard is an illustrator, animator, public speaker, and special education teacher who creates art to improve the awareness of learning differences and mental health.

Mads is the co-director & co-producer of the award-winning short film *I Am Dyslexic*, director and producer of short film *The whole Universe in My Suitcase* – an ADHD Norway short film – and illustrator of the book *There are words behind the letters* – a handbook for all individuals with dyslexia.

Made in the USA
Monee, IL
05 August 2021